ON VACATION

Written by Kiah Thomas

Illustrated by K-Fai Steele

NEAL PORTER BOOKS
HOLIDAY HOUSE / NEW YORK

Neal Porter Books

An imprint of Holiday House Publishing, Inc.
Edited by Taylor Norman

Text copyright © 2025 by Kiah Thomas
Illustrations copyright © 2025 by K-Fai Steele
All Rights Reserved
HOLIDAY HOUSE is registered in the U.S. Patent and Trademark Office.
Printed and bound in January 2025 at C&C Offset, Shenzhen, China.
The artwork was created with watercolor and pencil.
Book design by Jennifer Browne
www.holidayhouse.com
First Edition
1 3 5 7 9 10 8 6 4 2

This book was printed on FSC ® -certified text paper

Library of Congress Cataloging-in-Publication Data

Names: Thomas, Kiah, author. | Steele, K-Fai, illustrator.
Title: Lone wolf on vacation / written by Kiah Thomas ; illustrated by K-Fai Steele.
Description: First edition. | New York : Neal Porter Books / Holiday House, 2025. | Series: Lone wolf ; 3 | Audience: Ages 6–9 | Audience: Grades 2–3 | Summary: "Wolf's hope for a peaceful, solitary vacation are dashed when familiar faces turn up at his getaway locale"— Provided by publisher.
Identifiers: LCCN 2024018106 | ISBN 9780823457793 (hardcover)
Subjects: CYAC: Vacations—Fiction. | Humorous stories. | LCGFT: Humorous fiction. | Picture books.
Classification: LCC PZ7.1.T462 Loo 2025 | DDC [E]—dc23
LC record available at https://lccn.loc.gov/2024018106

ISBN: 978-0-8234-5779-3 (hardcover)

EU Authorized Representative: HackettFlynn Ltd., 36 Cloch Choirneal, Balrothery, Co. Dublin, K32 C942, Ireland. EU@walkerpublishinggroup.com

For Mum and Dad —K.T.

For Rich and Flo —K.S.

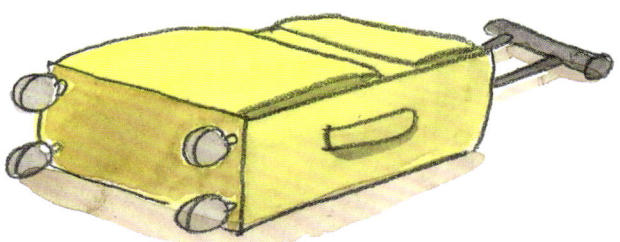

CHAPTER 1
Vacation

It was summer vacation.
Wolf packed his bags.
He watered his plants.
He said goodbye to . . .

NO ONE!

Wolf didn't have any friends to say goodbye to.
Which was just the way he liked it.

Wolf couldn't wait to go on vacation.

To smell the fresh air.

To see the sights.

To be alone in new places.

And best of all, he wouldn't have to worry about running into anyone he knew.

Wolf could feel himself relaxing already.

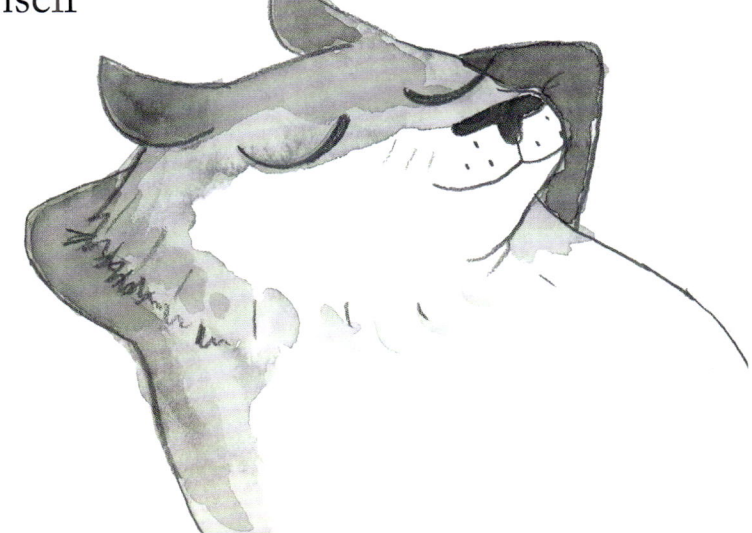

CHAPTER
2
The Bus

Wolf rode his bike to the bus stop. He decided to leave in the middle of the night so that there would be fewer people on the bus.

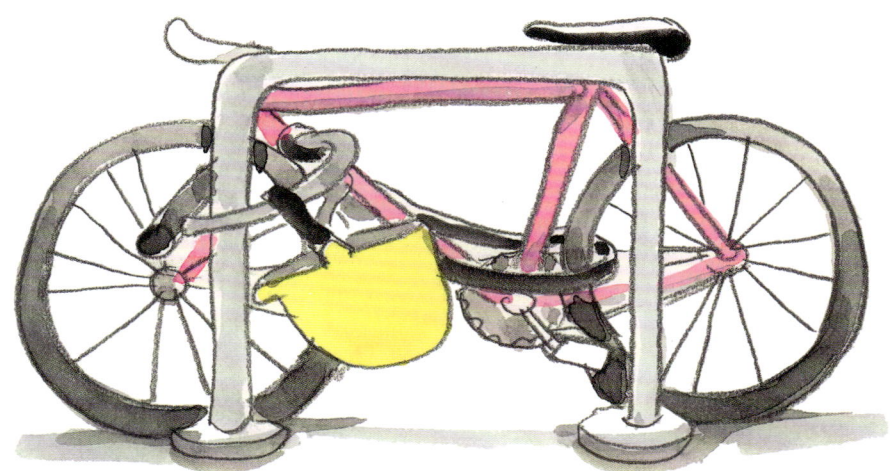

"Hello," said the quiet bus driver. The bus was empty apart from an angry boy in the back seat.

Wolf sat in the middle of the bus, away from the angry boy, but not too close to the quiet bus driver.

The bus was quiet.
It was the perfect start
to a solo vacation.

"How about a sing-along?" called the bus driver. *Oh no.*

This was not a quiet bus driver. This was a *singing* bus driver.

"*The wheels on the bus go round and round*," sang the singing bus driver.

"Grrrr!" said Wolf.

"*Round and round, round and round,*" sang the singing bus driver. "Come on, everybody now!"

"GRRRR!" said Wolf more loudly.

But the singing bus driver didn't hear him.

Because the angry boy at the back of the bus had joined in the singing.

"*The wheels on the bus go round and round,*" they sang from the front and the back.

Oh no. Oh no, no, no.

It was a singing bus driver *and* a singing boy.

"*All the way to town.*"

CHAPTER
3
The Hotel

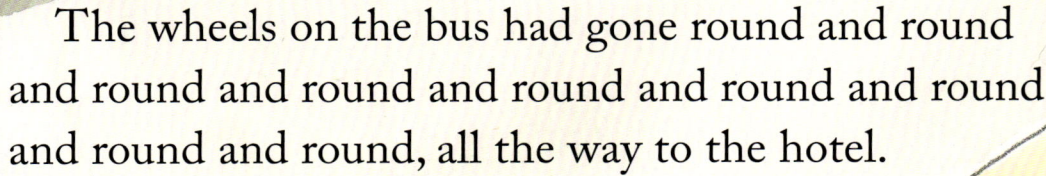

The wheels on the bus had gone round and round and round and round and round and round and round and round and round, all the way to the hotel.

Wolf had a headache.

He was looking forward to getting to his room.

He would lie on his bed. He would listen to the silence.

"Hiya!" said a cheery hotel receptionist.
"Grrrr," said Wolf.
"You must be Wolf!" said the cheery hotel receptionist.

"Here are your keys! You are in room 405. That's on level four! You will need to take the elevator."

The elevator was empty.

But just as the doors were about to close, a hand shot between them.

"Hello, Wolf!" said an eager girl. She hopped into the elevator. "I didn't know you were on vacation here! This place has the best elevators!"

Wolf was glad his room was only on level four. He watched the numbers go up.

1 . . .

2 . . .

3 . . .

3 . . .

3 . . .

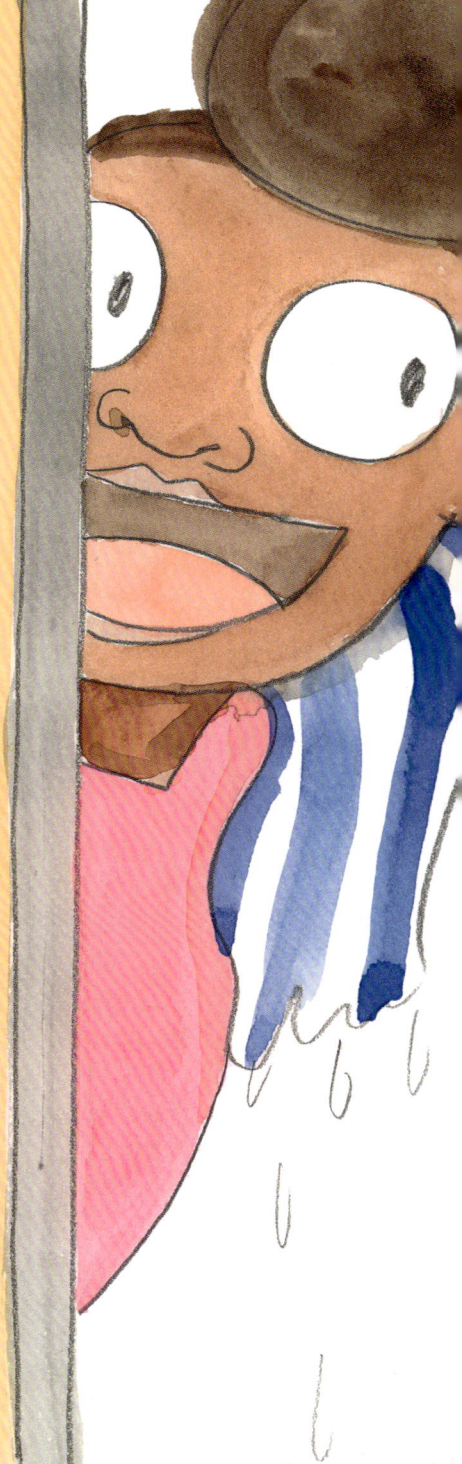

The elevator had stopped moving.

"The elevator seems to be stuck," said the eager girl. "But at least we are stuck together. Do you want to sing a song?"

"Grrrr!" said Wolf.

He pressed all the buttons.
Nothing worked.

Wolf picked up the emergency phone. "GRRRR!" he said.

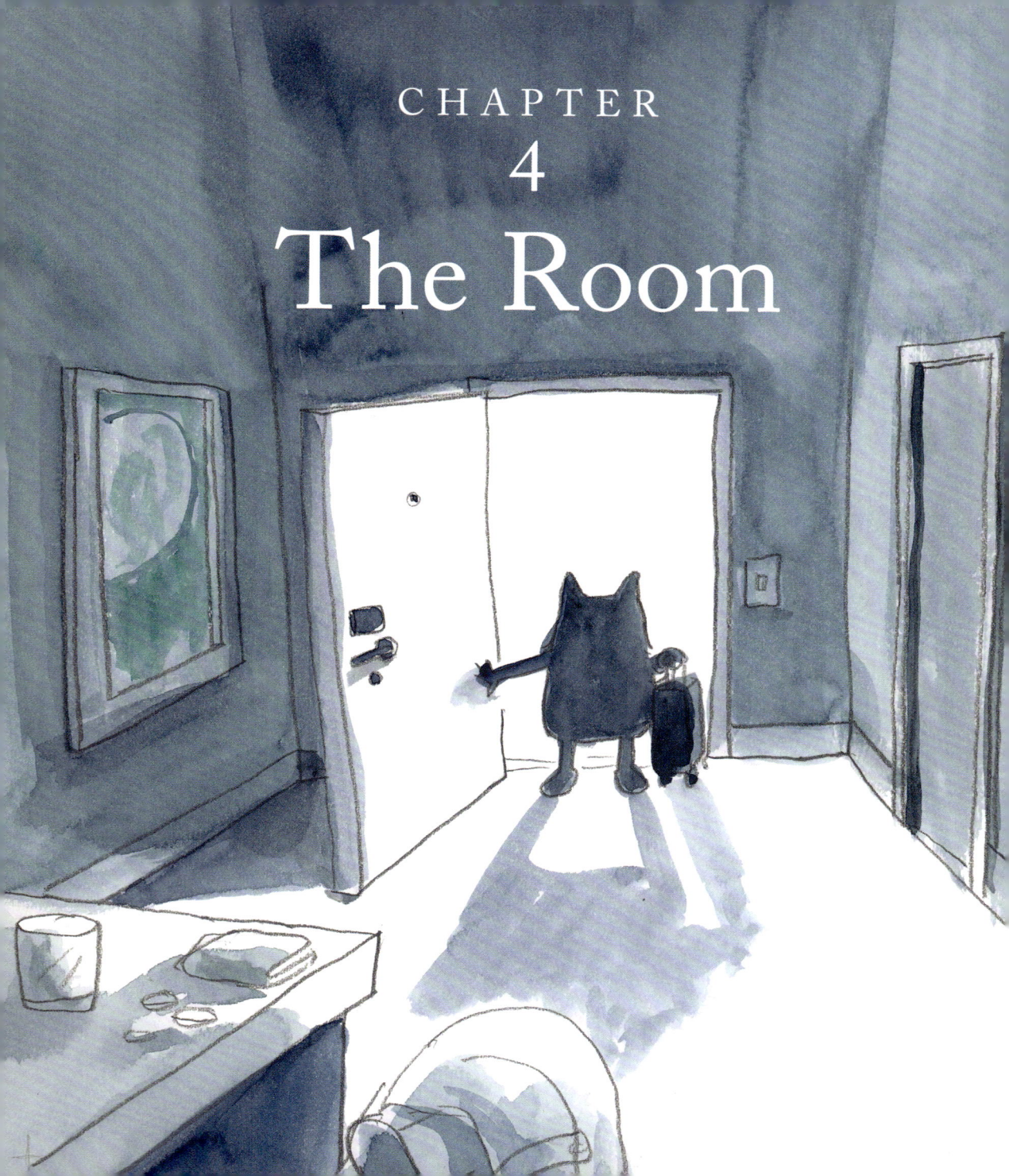

Wolf went to his bedroom.
He took off his shoes.
 He sat on the bed. The bed was lumpy.
 Wolf jumped up. There was someone in his room. There was someone sleeping in his *bed*!
 "Grrrr," said Wolf.

"Zzzz," said the sleeping someone.
"Grrrr!" said Wolf.

"Zzzz!" said the sleeping someone.
"GRRRR!" said Wolf.
The sleeping someone rolled over.
"ZZZZ!" they said.

Wolf didn't know what to do. He could not growl any louder. But he did not want to talk to the cheery receptionist again.
He would have to find somewhere else to sleep.

He lay down on a deck chair.
He closed his eyes.
If he fell asleep, it would *feel* like he was alone.

Splash!
Someone jumped in the pool.
Wolf felt a drop of water on his nose.

He breathed in. He breathed out. He did not growl.
He felt a drop of water on his ear. He felt a drop of water in his mouth.
Wolf opened his eyes.

"Hello, sleepyhead! You should come for a swim! This place has the best pools!"

A bossy boy stood above Wolf. He was where the drops had come from.

"Last one in is a rotten egg!"
said the bossy boy.

The bossy boy ran to the pool. If Wolf didn't move, he was going to get splashed again.
Wolf rolled off the deck chair and ran away.

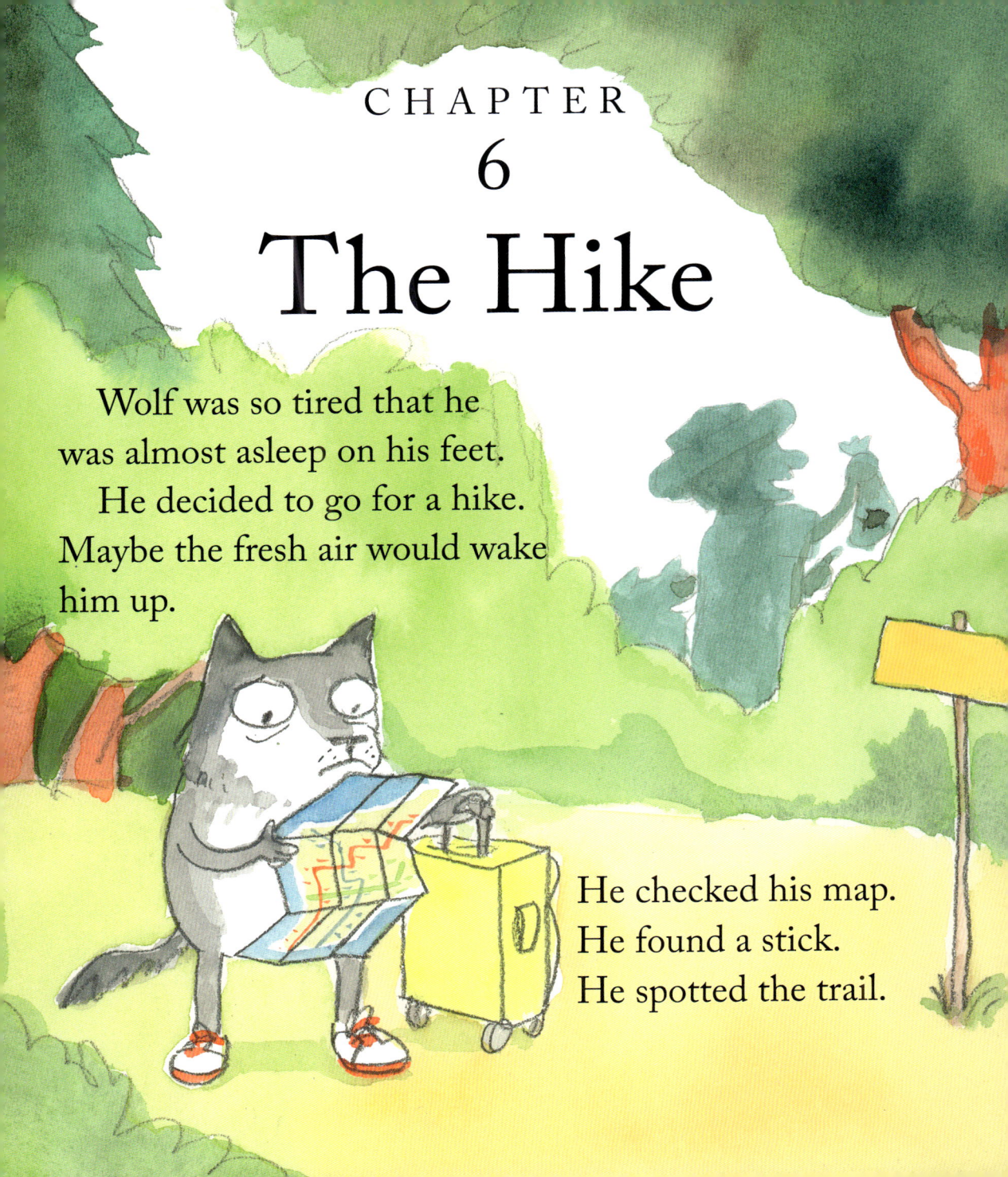

CHAPTER
6
The Hike

Wolf was so tired that he was almost asleep on his feet.
He decided to go for a hike. Maybe the fresh air would wake him up.

He checked his map.
He found a stick.
He spotted the trail.

But just as he was about to begin hiking, Wolf spotted something else.

A jolly hiker.

The jolly hiker started to turn around.

Wolf did not want to talk to the jolly hiker. Wolf did not even have enough energy to *growl* at the jolly hiker.

He threw a rock into the bushes.

"I say, what was that?" said the jolly hiker. He turned back to the bushes.

"This place has the best bushes!" he said.
Wolf ran in the opposite direction.

He walked down the road. This place had the best roads.

Wolf took a deep breath.

It was nice to be alone.

It reminded Wolf of the last time he had been alone.

And that gave Wolf an idea.

A bus passed by. There was singing out the window.
Wolf was glad he was not on the bus.
He kept walking.

CHAPTER
7
Vacation

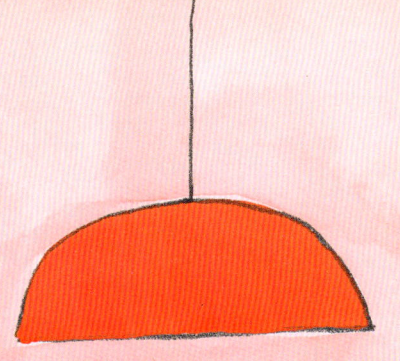

Wolf walked all the way home and straight into his very empty house.

There were no eager girls or bossy boys or jolly hikers.

Wolf was all alone.

He slept for three days.

It was a very nice vacation.

Read all the **LONE WOLF** books!

Lone Wolf Gets a Pet
Lone Wolf Goes to School
Lone Wolf Goes to the Library